GREAT PICTURES

AND THEIR STORIES

How To Look At Pictures

"You must look at pictures studiously, earnestly, honestly. It will take years before you come to a full appreciation of art; but when at last you have it, you will be possessed of the purest, loftiest and most ennobling pleasures that the civilized world can offer you."

JOHN C. VAN DYKE.

ST.
AA
PRESS

GREAT PICTURES
AND THEIR STORIES

INTERPRETING
MASTERPIECES
TO CHILDREN

BY
KATHERINE MORRIS LESTER

BOOK TWO

ST. AUGUSTINE ACADEMY PRESS

This book was originally published in 1927
by Mentzer, Bush & Company.

This facsimile edition reprinted in 2024
with improved color images
by St. Augustine Academy Press.

ISBN: 978-1-64051-145-3

CONTENTS

INDEX OF ILLUSTRATIONS IN GREAT PICTURES AND THEIR STORIES

FOREWORD

Picture Study is rapidly becoming an important factor in our public school education. "Nearly every progressive city," says the Bureau of Education, Washington, D. C., "is making use of some form of picture study in the public school system."

The twentieth century has ushered in the reproduction of masterpieces in color! To what heights of delight the children of the Public Schools may be carried by the famous pictures of the world in color!

It remains only for the elders to choose pictures adapted to the childish interests; pictures which will cultivate a taste for the best in art; pictures which through the impressionable early years will lead to a true understanding and appreciation of the world's masterpieces!

In preparing this series of readers it has been the aim of those selecting the pictures to consider always the child interest. The field of pictures is large. Not only have the "old masters" been drawn upon, but masters in modern art as well, including modern American artists. Thus constantly, through this series of pictures, the principles of beauty which made possible the "old masters" of yesterday are seen again in the art of today.

In the preparation of the text the child's interest and his ability to read are carefully considered. Real picture knowledge is conveyed in the child's own language.

In the primary grades the interest is largely in "what it is all about." Consequently the text aims to satisfy this curiosity, and at the same time lead to unconscious observation of those things which are most alive to the little child,—color, life, action.

The vocabulary for Books I, II, and III is based on "The Reading Vocabulary,"* the

*See Twenty-fourth Year Book, National Society for the Study of Education; Part I, 1925.

Horn, Horn, and Packer list of the Twenty-fourth Year Book.

In the intermediate grades, a lively interest in the story is always upper-most. Gradually an appreciation of picture-pattern develops. Simple elements in picture making,—i.e. center of interest, repetition of line and color,—may be intelligently comprehended by children of the intermediate grades.

In the grammar grades great interest in the story continues, and with this interest there develops an appreciation of HOW the story is told,—the real ART of the picture. The pupil not only learns that the picture is a masterpiece, but WHY. He thus acquires standards for judging other pictures.

Each picture is followed by a short sketch of the artist, told in a key adapted to the age and interest of the child.

The questions which follow the text will assist in developing an intelligent appreciation of the picture.

The author is particularly indebted to Miss Jennie Long, recently Supervisor of Primary Education, Peoria Public Schools, for valuable criticism of the primary text. Grateful acknowledgment is also made for the opportunity of practical work with a selected number of primary stories in the schools of Peoria.

The manuscripts of the intermediate and grammar grade books has been submitted to teachers of those grades, to whom the author is indebted for helpful practical suggestions.

The MUSICAL SELECTIONS for the pictures have been graciously contributed by Eva G. Kidder, Director of Music, Peoria Public Schools. The author believes this to be a very valuable feature of these books.

KATHERINE MORRIS LESTER.

ILLUSTRATED WITH REPRODUC-
TIONS IN COLOR FROM THE
ORIGINAL MASTERPIECES BY
COURTESY OF THE ART EXTEN-
SION SOCIETY OF NEW YORK

A HOLIDAY
Art Institute of Chicago

ARTIST: Edward H. Potthast
SCHOOL: American
DATES: 1857-1927

A HOLIDAY

A day full of sunlight!
A day full of fun!
Splash! Splash! Splash!

Water everywhere.
The waves roll in
    and dash about us.
What care we! We have come
    to the seashore to play.
This is our holiday!

It is such fun to play
    on a long sandy beach.
It is such fun to wade
    in the cool water.
Two, four, six, eight, ten!
Ten little children at the seashore!

The five little girls
　　wear their white summer dresses.
They keep close to shore.
One little girl dips the water
　　in her hands.
Another has a pretty red cup.

The little boy
　　is having a fine time.
He likes to wade far out.
His big yellow hat shades his face.
His green shirt is the same color
　　as the sky.

See the little girl
　　in the red cap!
She is very brave.
She goes far out
　　to meet the big rolling waves!

Near by are two other little girls.
They stand side by side
  in the water.
Their pet dog is with them.
He is very frisky.
He likes to run far out
  in the water.
He likes to dash and splash about!

See the bright sunlight! It shines
  upon the children's faces.
It shines upon their yellow hair.
It shines upon their white dresses.
It sparkles on the water.
It makes many colors
  in the water.
See the shadows!
They dance and ripple.
They ripple and dance!

What a wide, wide sea!
It goes far, far out.
There it meets the sky.
Far out the sea is very, very deep.
The water is dark, dark blue.

Roll! Roll! Roll!
See the white caps!
Splash! Splash!

The soft spray fills the air.
The sea rolls back.
The long sandy beach
 is even and smooth.

Can you tell the color
 of the sandy shore?
Can you tell the color
 of the shallow water?

The artist wanted a cool sea.
So he used cool color.
He used cool color
   for the "far" water.
He used cool color
   for the "near" water.
He used cool color
   for the sky.
Then he placed the warm sunshine
   over all.
This made a warm summer day
   at the seashore.

The breezes blow in from the sea.
The sunlight sparkles on the water.
Two, four, six, eight, ten!
Ten little children
   having a fine holiday
   at the seashore!

THE STORY OF THE ARTIST

This artist liked to paint sunlight.
He liked to paint children.

One day he walked
    by the seashore.
He saw these little girls
    in their pretty white dresses.
This was just the picture
    the artist wanted!
So he made this painting
    of a summer day
    at the seashore.
He called it, "A Holiday."

Today this picture hangs
    in the Art Institute of Chicago.
Many, many children go
    to see it every year.

SOMETHING TO TELL.

1. Did you ever play by the sea?
   What kind of a beach
      do you like best? Why?

2. What kind of a day is this?
   Where is the sun? Is it hot?

3. What colors make it cool?

4. Name the colors
      in the "near" water.
   Name the colors
      in the "far" water.

5. How many children do you see?
   Who is having the best time?

Related Music: SECOND GAVOTTE....
   ....*Sapellnikoff*
   O SOLE MIO...........
   ......*Neapolitan Folk Song*

MADAME LEBRUN AND HER DAUGHTER
The Louvre, Paris

ARTIST: Madame Vigee-Lebrun
SCHOOL: French
DATES: 1755-1842

MOTHER AND DAUGHTER

Once there was a little girl.
Her name was Jeanne.
She lived far across the ocean.
She lived in France.
She was a little French girl.

Jeanne's mother was an artist.
She painted the pictures
  of kings and queens.
She painted this picture
  of little Jeanne.

One day she thought to herself,
  "I must have a picture
  of my dear little Jeanne."
Just then the door opened,
  and in ran little Jeanne.

She ran to her mother
　　and threw her arms
　　about her neck.
"Oh, mother! I love you so!"
　　said little Jeanne.

A mirror was hanging on the wall.
Mother happened to look
　　into the mirror.
There she saw the pretty picture
　　that she and little Jeanne made.

"This is just the picture for me
　　to make!" said the mother.
"Yes, yes! mother, do!"
　　cried little Jeanne.
"I will stand as still
　　as still can be
　　while you paint my picture."

Soon the mother began to draw.

She drew for a few minutes.

Then she and little Jeanne
  looked into the mirror.

By and by, after many days,
  the picture was finished.

See the pretty colors!

Jeanne's dress is blue-green.

Mother's dress is white.

She wears a pretty red sash.

The red sash and blue-green dress
  are beautiful side by side.

A golden-brown robe
  lies upon mother's lap.

She wears a red ribbon in her hair.

It is the same color as the sash.

She has big beautiful eyes,
  and a lovely face.

Little Jeanne is beautiful, too.
Her mother said she had
  "one of the sweetest faces
  to be seen."
She has pretty blue eyes,
  a little mouth,
  and soft curling hair.

See how Jeanne's arm curves
  with mother's arm!
See how Jeanne's head rests
  beside mother's cheek.
This makes a beautiful picture.

Perhaps we can make a picture
  like little Jeanne
  and her mother.
Who will be the mother?
Who will be little Jeanne?

Mother will sit very still.
Jeanne must run in
  and throw her arms
  about her mother's neck.
What a beautiful picture
  of mother and daughter we make!

THE STORY OF THE ARTIST

Jeanne's mother began to paint
  when she was a very little girl.
Her father was an artist.
He gave the little girl
  her first lessons
  in drawing and painting.
She painted so well
  that her father was delighted.
One day he said to her,
  "You will be a great artist
  if ever there was one."

And she did grow up to be
  one of the greatest painters
  of France.

Everybody loved Jeanne.
Everybody loved Jeanne's mother.
Her name was Madame Lebrun.
This picture of little Jeanne
  and her mother
  is over one hundred years old.
It hangs in a beautiful palace
  far, far across the sea.
Some day you may sail
  over the sea.
You may see this picture
  of Jeanne and her mother.
You will find little Jeanne
  looking just as happy
  as she does in our picture!

SOMETHING TO TELL.

1. How did the artist happen
   to paint this picture?

2. What color is Jeanne's hair?
   What color is Jeanne's dress?
   What color is mother's dress?
   What color is mother's sash?
   What colors are pretty
     side by side?

3. Where do you see pretty curves?
   Do you like them? Why?

4. Can you tell the artist's name?

5. Do you like the picture? Why?

Related Music: ADORATION....*Borowski*

27

DON BALTHAZAR CARLOS

Far, far, across the ocean
   there is a land
   where the sun is always shining.
This land is "Sunny Spain."
The people in Spain are very happy.
They do not work hard.
They spend their time in games
   and other pleasures.

Once there was a king of Spain.
He was called King Philip.
This king had a little son.
He was six years old.
His name
   was Don Balthazar Carlos.
What a big name
   for such a little boy!

DON BALTHAZAR CARLOS
Prado, Madrid

ARTIST: Don Rodriquez de Silva y Velasquez
SCHOOL: Spanish
DATES: 1599-1660

This little prince liked to do
　　just as his father, the king, did.
He saw his father go out to ride
　　upon his prancing steed.
He, too, wanted to ride!

"Our little prince
　　must learn to ride," said the king,
　　"then he shall have a fine new pony."
So Don Carlos went to riding school.
There he learned to sit
　　in the saddle
　　like a little man.

But little boys, six years old,
　　must not ride frisky ponies!
No! No! No! His father was careful
　　to get a pony
　　that could not run away!

One day a present came
  to the palace for the prince.
It was a plump little pony!

See the little prince
  on his new chestnut pony!
He looks very fine
  as he gallops along.
He wants to ride
  just as his father rides.
His father
  was "The best rider in Spain."

Don Carlos wears his best clothes.
His jacket is dark, rich velvet.
His sleeves are silk.
See the high boots!
His silken scarf flies to the breeze!
How fast he gallops along!

See the handsome hat! It is set
  on one side of his head.
See the fine driving gloves!
Yes! Don Carlos is a prince!
A prince must wear gloves!

He carries a baton in his hand.
We often saw his father, the king,
  carry a baton.
He is very proud to do
  just as his father does.

The new pony is so little.
He is round as a ball.
He could not run away!
No! No! No! He is too plump!
The king was very wise. He knew
  that just such a pony as this
  was best for a small boy of six.

When the artist made this picture
   of the little prince, he painted
   a beautiful background.
See the soft gray clouds!
See the low green hills!
Beyond, are the mountains.

See the pretty white snow
   on the very tip-top
   of the mountain!
These colors are soft and gray.
They make a beautiful background
   for the little prince
   and his pony.

On he gallops!
This little Spanish rider!
What fun it is to be a prince
   and ride a fine new pony!

THE STORY OF THE ARTIST.

This artist made many pictures
  of the little prince.
He painted this picture
  as a present for the king.
The king was very happy. He kept it
  in his palace for many years.
Now many people go to Spain
  to see this painting
  of the little prince
  upon his fine new pony.

The king invited the artist
  to live in his palace.
There the artist painted pictures
  of all the king's children.
He is one of the great painters
  of the world.
His name is Velasquez.

SOMETHING TO TELL

1. Do you like to ride a pony?

2. Do you like this pony? Why?
   Do you think he will run away?

3. Where does this little boy live?
   What is his name?
   Why does he like to ride?

4. What is the color of his jacket?
   Why does he carry a baton?

5. Why is the background
   soft and gray?
   Do you like the picture? Why?

Related Music: THE LITTLE HUNTSMAN
.........*French Folk Song*
MY PONY..*Grant-Schaefer*

BOY WITH A RABBIT
Burlington House, London

ARTIST: Sir Henry Raeburn
SCHOOL: English
DATES: 1756-1823

THE BOY WITH A RABBIT

Who has a pretty white rabbit?
Who will have his picture painted
  with a pretty white rabbit?

Once upon a time
  there was a little boy.
He lived in Scotland.
His father gave him many pets.
He had a pony, a dog, a parrot,
  and a rabbit.

It was a beautiful rabbit.
It had pink eyes, and long ears
  lined with pink.
The pink eyes and pink ears
  were very pretty colors
  with the soft white fur.

One day an artist saw the boy
  with his little pet rabbit.
"Ah! a new picture!" he exclaimed.
The little boy was delighted.

He dressed himself
  in his prettiest clothes.
He put on his shirt of soft white.
It had long sleeves
  and cuffs of white.
It had a V-shaped neck.
It had a pretty frill
  about the neck.

He wore long trousers.
He set a little cap on one side
  of his head.
He carried his rabbit. He was ready
  for his picture.

This artist loved the skies
  of Scotland.
He loved the trees, too.
"We must make our picture
  with the sky in the distance,"
  said the artist. "We must have
  a place for bunny, too."
"Oh, yes!" said the little boy,
  "I want my bunny beside me."

Soon the little boy sat down
  beside a low tree-trunk.
The artist put some green leaves
  on the tree-trunk.
Then he placed the rabbit
  beside the green leaves.
The little boy placed his arm
  about bunny.
This made a beautiful picture.

The rabbit sat very still
  as he nibbled the green leaves.
The little boy sat very still
  as he watched the artist work.
Soon the picture was finished.

The little boy has a lovely face.
He has large, brown eyes
  and a pretty mouth.
His hair is dark.

The light shines
  upon the white shirt.
This makes the shirt very light
  in many places.
The pretty, white rabbit is as light
  as the bright spots
  on the shirt.
His eyes are dark.

The artist wanted the boy's face
  to be the lightest part
  of the picture.
So he made the background very dark.
The cap is dark, too. This makes
  the beautiful face shine out.

All about the picture
  is fine, soft air. The soft air
  is all about the little boy
  and his rabbit.
This makes the picture beautiful.

THE STORY OF THE ARTIST

A long time ago
  there was another little boy.
He was a little orphan boy.
He, too, lived in Scotland.
His name was Henry Raeburn.

This little orphan boy
   lived in a big house
   with other orphan children.
There he learned
   to read, write, and spell.
He learned a little drawing, too.

As he grew older, he began to paint.
He painted little faces.
By and by he became a great painter.
The king became his friend.
The king was very proud of him.
He made him a knight.

So the little orphan boy
   became a knight.
He became the greatest painter
   in Scotland.
"The Boy with a Rabbit"
   is one of his best pictures.

SOMETHING TO TELL

1. Did you ever have a pet rabbit?
   What was its color?

2. Where does this little boy live?
   What was his favorite pet?

3. How did he pose for his picture?

4. What kind of a shirt does he wear?
   What kind of a cap does he wear?

5. What is the lightest part
   of the picture?
   Why did the artist make it light?
   Why is the background dark?

Related Music: THE SWAN....*Saint Saens*
TO A WILD ROSE......
...............*MacDowell*

THE STORAGE ROOM
Rijksmuseum, Amsterdam

ARTIST: Pieter de Hooch
SCHOOL: Dutch
DATES: 1629-1677

THE STORAGE ROOM

What a pretty Dutch house!
This is a house in Holland.
The little Dutch girl has come
    for her pitcher of milk.

"Oh, yes!" said the Dutch woman,
    "I have your pitcher of milk.
    It has been in the storage room
    since morning."
Then she opened the door
    of the cool storage room.
We can see the end of the barrel
    that holds the milk.
Here is where the Dutch woman
    keeps all good things to eat.
Cheese, butter, eggs, and milk
    are kept in the storage room.

The Dutch woman gives the milk
   to the little girl.
See how she takes hold
   of the pitcher!
How careful she is!
It is a big pitcher
   for her little hands. But she
   will carry it home to mother.

What a strange dress
   the little girl wears!
It is very long.
All little girls in Holland
   wear long dresses.
She wears a white collar and cuffs.
She wears a little Dutch bonnet.
We cannot see her shoes.
Do you know what kind of shoes
   little Dutch children wear?

The Dutch woman wears a bonnet.

Her dress is pinned up.

Her blouse is red and green
   like the squares in the floor.

She is very happy.

The little girl is happy, too.

A pitcher of fresh milk
   means a cool drink
   when she reaches home.

See the sunlight!

It is golden yellow.

It comes streaming in
   through the pretty Dutch windows.

It turns the walls
   to bright warm yellow.

It fills the air with yellow light.

It brightens up the pretty squares
   in the floor.

See the blue cushion on the chair!
Here is where the sun is brightest!
Here is where the Dutch woman
   likes to sit and sew.
Dutch houses are so very queer.
They have tiled floors.
They have beamed ceilings.
They have pretty windows
   with many little panes.
The artist who painted our picture
   liked to have many open doors
   in his pictures.

In this picture he opened two doors.
We see two other rooms.
But we like the big room best.
The Dutch woman and the little girl
   make a pretty pattern
   against the warm, yellow wall.

Soon the little girl
will be going home.
She will carry her pitcher
of fresh milk to mother.

THE STORY OF THE ARTIST

This picture was painted
by a Dutchman.
He lived in Holland
over two hundred years ago.
He painted many pictures
of Dutch houses.
He painted many pictures
of Dutch children.
Today many boys and girls
read about his pictures.
He liked best of all to paint
golden sunshine, streaming
through pretty Dutch windows.

49

He liked to fill his Dutch houses
  with warm yellow light.
He liked to see the sunlight
  on the walls.
He liked to see it
  dancing on the floor.
He liked to have many open doors
  in his pictures.
Sometimes the doors open
  into other rooms.
Sometimes they open into a garden.
Sometimes they open into a street.
Sometimes we see a Dutch canal
  through the open doorway.
Wherever the door opens
  it always leads out
  into the full sunlight—
  the bright, beautiful sunlight
  of Holland!

SOMETHING TO TELL

1. Where is this little house?
   How many rooms do you see?
   Where is the sunshine brightest?

2. What kind of floors
      have Dutch houses?
   What kind of ceilings? Windows?

3. How is the little girl dressed?
   How is the woman dressed?

4. Why does the artist place them
      in front of the light wall?

5. What did he like best to paint?

Related Music: MUSETTE ....*Gluck*

THE PASTRY EATERS
Munich Gallery

ARTIST: Bartolomé Esteban Murillo
SCHOOL: Spanish
DATES: 1616-1682

THE PASTRY EATERS

Who are these little boys
  with the dark faces?
Where do they live?
What are they doing?

They are little Spanish boys.
They live in "Sunny Spain."
It is very hot in Spain.
The people spend most of the time
  out-of-doors.

Many of the people are very poor.
They often live a whole day
  upon a crust of bread.
Many of the children beg
  upon the streets.
Sometimes they earn a few pennies
  by selling fruits and flowers.

These little Spanish boys
   live all day in the bright sunshine.
How dark is their skin!
They wear no hats.
They wear no shoes.
Their clothes are poor and ragged.

They have been selling fruit.
Now they rest by the roadside,
   and have something to eat.
They are eating pastry.

Pastry is a very soft bread.
It is made of flour and water.
One little boy holds
   a piece of pastry above his head.
He will soon catch it in his mouth.
The other boy smiles.
He thinks it's lots of fun.

Their good friend, the dog,
   has been with them all day.
He, too, is hungry.
Soon he will speak for his dinner.
How he watches the pastry!
See the three heads! First boy,
   second boy, and the dog!
All three watching the pastry!

Perhaps the artist walked
   along this road
   while the boys were resting.
He could always see a picture
   when Spanish boys sat together.
This made a pretty picture for him.
He saw all the lovely color
   in the boys' faces.
He saw all the rich color
   in their poor clothes.

55

He saw the pretty yellow
  of the basket.
He saw the soft color
  of the fruit, too.
He put all the colors together
  and made a beautiful picture.

See the color of the dog!
I think friend dog has caught
  all the sunshine in Spain!
Don't you?

THE STORY OF THE ARTIST

This artist painted many pictures
  of the poor children of Spain.
Sometimes they are counting
  their pennies.
Sometimes they are eating
  melons and fruits.

He always painted real children
because he saw them every day
in sunny Spain.

This painter was born in Spain.
His name is Murillo.
When he was a little boy
he was very poor. He was as poor
as the little beggar boys
he painted.
When he grew to be a man,
he took his paints, his brushes,
and his easel
to the market-place.
This was where all the people
came to buy food and clothing.
Here he saw many beggar children.
Here he painted them as they sat
in the market-place.

By and by he painted many pictures
   for the churches of Spain.
These were beautiful pictures
   of the Christ-Child
   and his Mother.
Today these pictures
   are among the famous pictures
   of the world.
The people of Spain
   are very proud
   of their great painter.
Though he lived so long ago,
   they will never forget him.
On Sundays and holidays
   crowds of men, women,
   and children go
   to the great galleries
   to see the famous pictures
   of Murillo.

SOMETHING TO TELL

1. Where do these little boys live?
   Are they rich or poor?

2. What is the color of their faces?
   What is the color of their hair?

3. What are they doing now?

4. What is most important
     in the picture?
   How can you tell?

5. What is the color of sunlight?
   What color has the artist
     used most? Why?

Related Music: RONDINO ON THEME..
....*Beethoven*
A SONG WITHOUT
     WORDS ....*Just*

THE AGE OF INNOCENCE
National Gallery, London

ARTIST: Sir Joshua Reynolds
SCHOOL: English
DATES: 1723-1792

THE AGE OF INNOCENCE

Once upon a time a great artist
  lived in England.
He was the painter of children.
His name was Sir Joshua Reynolds.

No one ever painted more children
  than he did.
All the children were his friends.
They liked to visit him
  in his big country house.
Here he had one large room.
It was called, "The Studio."
In the studio he kept many toys.
Big toys! Little toys!
He kept birds and other pets, too.
No wonder the children
  liked to visit the artist!

Sir Joshua was a true friend
   to all the children.
He was delighted to have them
   come to his house in the country.
He played games with them.
He told them wonderful stories.
He took them out to ride.
Oh, they had such jolly times
   when they visited the artist!

Sir Joshua had a little grand-niece.
Her name was Theophilia.
Everybody called her "Offy."
Offy was a dear little girl.
One day she came to visit her uncle.
She was just six years old.
She looked so sweet and lovely
   that the artist
   wanted to paint her picture.

Offy was delighted
   to have her picture painted.
She sat down under a big tree
   and folded her hands
   on her breast.
She wore a light yellow dress.
Her hair was tied
   with a yellow ribbon.
The ribbon was the same color
   as the dress.
Her little feet were bare.
The artist liked best to see
   the side of Offy's pretty head.
So he turned her head.

Offy sat still, oh, so very still,
   for a long time.
Perhaps she had to pose many days
   before her picture was finished.

See her pretty childish nose
  and baby mouth!
See her beautiful hair! It curls
  over her forehead and ears.

Do you see the big tree?
It is very shady under the tree.
Offy's dress is very light.
See the light pattern it makes
  against the dark background!
Away off in the distance we see
  the blue sky and sunset colors.

Little Offy looked so lovely!
She looked innocent
  as all little children look.
The artist was so pleased
  that he called his picture,
  "The Age of Innocence."

Everybody likes
   "THE AGE OF INNOCENCE."
It hangs in a large picture gallery
   in London.
Many people go to see it every day.

Come! Let us go into the garden!
Who will pose like Offy
   for her picture?
If you do, you must turn your head
   to one side. You must fold
   your hands on your breast,
   just as Offy did.
We must see your little bare feet
   under the edge of your dress.
Come! Let us go into the garden!
Who will pose like Offy
   for her picture?

65

THE STORY OF THE ARTIST

When Sir Joshua was a little boy
 he was always drawing pictures.
At school he drew many pictures
 on his lesson papers.
Sometimes he drew funny pictures.
They made the children laugh.

When Joshua was eleven years old,
 he painted a picture of a man.
He showed it to his father.
His father said—"It is wonderful.
 Joshua must have lessons
 in drawing and painting."
So Joshua began to study.
By and by he grew to be
 a very great painter.
He became known far and wide
 as "The Painter of Children."

SOMETHING TO TELL

1. What is the little girl's name?
   How is she dressed?

2. How does she pose
   for her picture?

3. Why did the artist
   like the light dress?

4. Can you tell the artist's name?
   Did he like children?

5. What kind of pictures
   did he paint most?

Related Music: MORNING ....*Grieg*
               TRAUMEREI ...*Schumann*
               SIMPLE CONFESSION..
               ....*Thome*

HOME WORK
Collection Gallinard, Parish

ARTIST: Eugene Carrière
SCHOOL: French
DATES: 1849-1906

HOME WORK

Three happy children
  with a big open book!
They are sitting at the table
  with the open book before them.

How the baby listens
  to all big brother says!
How sister looks over the pages
  as brother talks!
All three are happy with the book.

Our picture is called, "Home Work."
Perhaps the children are studying
  their school lessons.
Perhaps they are only amusing
  themselves with the stories
  and pictures of the big book.

All three are thinking
about the book.
One little girl is older
and understands far more
than the other.
Perhaps brother is telling baby
about the story that he reads.
She is very quiet. Her little hands
are folded on the table.
How she listens! How she thinks!
Nobody knows just what baby thinks!

What bright, happy faces they are!
Yes, and each is different.
Brother's face is very kind.
He has large brown eyes
and dark brown hair.
Sister's face is very thoughtful.
She, too, has large brown eyes.

Baby's face is very earnest.
She has such a little nose.
She has such a little mouth.
She does not say a word.
She only listens to the story.
She wants to hear every word
  big brother has to say!

See the happy faces! How they shine
  out of the dark background!
Do you see
  that baby wears a light dress?
Do you see that brother and sister
  are in very dark color?
Baby, the book, the hands,
  and the three little faces
  are the only light spots
  in the picture.
All else is dark, very dark.

The three faces and the near edges
of the book
make a little path of light
around the picture.
The path is like a long circle.
Can you swing the circle
round and round?
Round and round
swings the little path of light!
It makes a pattern of light
against the dark background.
The artist thought very much
about his pattern.
He knew the dark background
would make the three faces
shine out.
He knew this would help us to see
only the three happy faces
of the children.

THE STORY OF THE ARTIST

This artist liked best of all
  to paint in soft dark colors.
He liked dark browns and yellows.
Sometimes faces look very pale
  as they shine out
  of the dark background.

This painter lived in France.
When he was a little boy
  he liked best to draw and paint.
When he grew to be a man, he wanted,
  oh, so much, to be a painter.

He began to study pictures.
He liked best
  the pictures of the Dutch painters.
He learned many things
  from the Dutch painters.

He learned how to make
  backgrounds very dark.
He learned how to keep faces light.
By and by he began to paint
  as the Dutch artists painted.

Everybody liked his pictures.
They liked to see the faces shine
  out of the dark background.
They liked the pattern of light
  against dark.
They liked his beautiful colors.

Many times this artist painted
  pictures of his own children.
Perhaps the three children
  in our picture, "Home Work,"
  are his own little family.

SOMETHING TO TELL

1. Have you a little brother
   or sister?
   Do you ever sit about a table
   with a big book?

2. How old is baby?
   How old is sister?
   How old is brother?

3. Why is the background dark?

4. Where is the little path
   of light?

5. What do you like best
   about the picture?

Related Music: CHANT D'AUTOMNE...
............*Tschaikowsky*

CHILDREN OF CHARLES I
Turin Gallery

ARTIST: Sir Anthony Van Dyck
SCHOOL: Flemish
DATES: 1599-1641

CHILDREN OF CHARLES I.

Once upon a time there was a king.

He had three beautiful children.

He loved his children very much.

One day he invited a great artist
to paint their pictures.

The artist painted many pictures
of the king's children.

Our picture is the most beautiful
of them all.

Here stands the Princess Mary
with her two baby brothers.

The big brother is Prince Charles.

The baby is Prince James.

Prince James is often called
"Baby Stuart."

Have you ever seen a picture
of Baby Stuart?

See the beautiful dresses!
They are silk and lace.
Babies never wear such dresses now!
But these are the king's children.
The king's children must have
   the most beautiful dresses
   in all the world!
See Prince Charles!
He is only five years old.
See his pretty dress!
It is rose-colored silk and lace.
My, my, my! How could
   the little prince walk about
   in such a long and fancy dress?
See the little bonnet he wears!
See the wonderful lace collar
   and cuffs! They are like
   the collar and cuffs
   of his father, the king.

His big collie dog sits beside him.
Prince Charles places his hand
　on the dog's head.
Friend Collie wonders
　what it is all about.
Prince James is only two years old.
He is so little he must stand
　on a platform.
Now he is taller!
What a dear little baby prince
　he is!
See his pretty little head!
See his pretty round face!
He holds a big round ball
　in his hands.
He wears a wonderful dress
　of blue silk. He wears lace cuffs,
　and a little bonnet. The bonnet
　is tied under his chin.

Princess Mary
   looks just like a little queen.
She is four years old.
Her dress is white silk.
See how very long it is!
Oh, yes! She must have a dress
   like that of her mother,
   the queen!
Princess Mary does not wear a cap
   upon her pretty head.
She is very proud
   of her beautiful curls.
She wants all the world to see them.
See the dark curtain
   at the back of the picture!
The artist made it very dark.
He knew that the dark background
   would make the pretty faces
   and beautiful dresses shine out.

He put the dark rose-bush
   back of Baby Stuart
   so we could see
   his dear little baby head.
Above the rose-bush
   is a peep of blue sky.
I think some of the roses
   from the bush
   are lying on the floor,
   don't you?
See how the light shines
   on the children!
See how it shines
   on their pretty silk dresses!
How it lights their pretty faces!
This is just as the artist wished.
He wanted us to see
   only the three beautiful children
   of the king!

THE STORY OF THE ARTIST

The artist was the king's friend.
He painted pictures of the king
  and queen. He painted pictures
  of all of the king's children.
When he was a little boy,
  his father owned a silk store.
Here he first learned
  to like the pretty silks.
Here he first saw the light
  play over their pretty folds.
When he grew up he liked best of all
  to paint people
  in dresses of silk, satin, and lace.
I must tell you the artist's name.
It is Sir Anthony Van Dyck.
He is one of the greatest artists
  of the world.

SOMETHING TO TELL

1. Who are these pretty children?
   Give their names.

2. How old is Princess Mary?
   How old is Prince Charles?
   How old is Prince James?

3. Name the colors in their clothes.
   Whose dress do you like best?

4. Why did the artist use
      the dark curtain?

5. Who is the artist?
   What did he like best to paint?

Related Music: AIR DE BALLET.......
......................*Jadossohn*

83

THE SISTINE MADONNA

A beautiful Mother!
A beautiful Child!
This is the Christ-Child
   and his Mother.
See the wonderful face
   of the Christ-Child!
See the beautiful face
   of the Mother!
They are coming down
   from heaven to earth.
See how the breeze
   fills out the Mother's scarf!
This picture was painted long ago.
Long ago people could not read
   the stories of the Christ-Child
   and his Mother. They had no books
   as we have today.

SISTINE MADONNA
Dresden Gallery

ARTIST: Raphael Sanzio
SCHOOL: Italian
DATES: 1483-1520

But one day the artists began
to paint. They began to paint
the stories of the Christ-Child
and his Mother.
Sometimes they painted
the story of his birthday.
Sometimes they painted
the story of the gifts
the Wise Men brought.
Sometimes they painted
only the Child and his Mother.
These pictures were placed
in the churches
for all the people to see.
The people read the picture
instead of a book. The picture
taught them many things
about the Child. It taught them
many things about the Mother, too.

In our picture the green curtains
   are drawn back. Now we may see
   the Mother and Child
   coming down to earth.
See the Child!
His eyes are wonderful.
They are so large! They see so far!
I think he sees all the children
   in the whole wide world!
His baby forehead
   rests against his mother's cheek.
The two faces
   are almost side by side.
The mother is beautiful.
Her eyes are large.
She seems to see away, way off.
Perhaps she, too, sees all the children
   in the whole wide world!

She wears a red dress.

About her sleeve is a band of gold.

She wears a white veil
about her shoulders. Her long scarf
is carried out like a sail.

Do you see the golden background?

Do you see the angel faces
about the Mother's head?

Oh, yes! All the golden background
is filled with angel faces!

They are singing songs of joy.

They know this is the Christ-Child
and His Mother!

The Christ-Child hears the singing.

He listens to their song.

The Mother seems to hear, too.

The angels must be singing
about the wonderful Child
and his Mother!

THE STORY OF THE ARTIST

This artist is one
   of the great painters of the world.
His name is Raphael.

Raphael's father
   was his first drawing teacher.
He taught him
   how to mix colors.
He taught him how to care
   for his brushes.
By and by Raphael went to study
   with a great artist. Soon he did
   better work than his teacher.
Soon he was known far and wide.
Everybody loved Raphael.
He was always kind and pleasant.
He did all he could
   to help other artists.
The king and queen were his friends.

They asked him many times
  to come to the palace.
Whenever Raphael went to the palace
  to see the king and queen,
    many of his friends went with him.
There were so many friends!
They made a great parade!
When the people
  saw this great parade, they knew
  that Raphael's friends loved him.
Raphael painted the walls
  of the king's palaces.
He painted the walls
  of the great churches.
He painted many beautiful pictures
  of the Christ-Child
  and his Mother.
The most beautiful of all
  is "The Sistine Madonna."

SOMETHING TO TELL

1. Who is the beautiful
   Mother and Child?
   How do you know
      they are coming down to earth?

2. Name the colors
      in the mother's dress.

3. What do you see
      in the background?

4. Of what is the Child thinking?
   Of what is the Mother thinking?

5. Do you like the picture? Why?

Related Music: JESU BAMBINO......*Yon*
                SONG OF THE CHIMES.
                      ....*Worrell*

PRONUNCIATION OF PROPER NAMES

CARRIERE .... (kä′ rē′ āir′)

DE HOOCH .... (dā hōk′)

MURILLO .... (mōō rē′ lyō)

POTTHAST .... (pŏt′ ăst)

RAEBURN .... (rā′ burn)

RAPHAEL .... (răf′ ā-ĕl)

REYNOLDS .... (rĕn′ ŭlds)

VELASQUEZ .... (vā lās′ kĕth)

VIGÉE-LEBRUN ....
.... (vī-gā lē-brŭn′)

DON BALTHASAR CARLOS
... (dŏn băl thăz′ är kär′ lōs)

SUGGESTIONS TO TEACHERS

STUDYING THE PICTURE. Any picture presented for study becomes more interesting when freely discussed in a natural way by the class. Before reading the text it is always advisable to study the picture. Pupils should be encouraged to give their own impressions; tell what they like in a picture, and WHY they like it.

In the primary grades the story interest is uppermost,—"what is it all about?" By tactful questioning the teacher may bring out many artistic points for observation. She may speak of color and action as well as story content. She may lead the pupil to discover new words which will appear in the text. These may be emphasized, written upon the board and studied. Thus they are greeted like old friends when met in the story.

DRAMATIZATION. In the p r i m a r y grades many pictures lend themselves to dramatization. With little children the "acting out" of the picture is a real joy. Under no circumstances is it necessary to burden one's self with an EXACT reproduction in the class room. The details of costume are not required. Any outstanding accessory, however, easily at hand, may add interest. It is the EFFORT on the part of the child to reproduce the pose and action that is of value. Frequently, if time permits, children may take turns in posing, letting the class decide who does best. Thus in a simple and direct way, many of the pictures selected for primary study may be given an added interest and charm.

CORRELATION. Language lessons both oral and written may be based on the work in picture-study. The questions following each picture, when answered either orally or in written form, necessitate close observation and intelligent expression.

As far as possible, each child should own his own pictures. This leads to the making of picture-study books, envelopes, folders, calendars, and other simple projects which utilize and also preserve the pictures.

The music hour offers still another opportunity for related study. Pictures, like music, create emotions. When possible in the study of pictures, add the music which may suggest the spirit and atmosphere of the picture. THE INTEREST IS ALWAYS KEENLY STIMULATED WHEN PORTIONS FROM VARIOUS SELECTIONS ARE PLAYED, AND THE CHILDREN PERMITTED TO CHOOSE THE ONE BEST SUITED TO THE PICTURE.

The suggestions for musical selections which follow the questions on the picture will be of great value to the teacher.

To be introduced in the early years to the masterpieces of the ages, and to learn of the kingly minds who have ruled in this realm of beauty, is sure to develop an interest which will enlarge, enrich, and refine the future life of the pupil.